the tale of a black cat

adapted by Carl Withers

illustrated by Alan Cober

holt, rinehart and winston / new york   chicago   san francisco

Books for Young Readers
by Carl Withers

The Tale of a Black Cat
I Saw a Rocket Walk a Mile
A Rocket in My Pocket

T.

Once there was a little boy named Tommy. And there's a That stands for Tommy.

Tommy's house was
not a very good one.
So he built a new wall
on this side of it.

And then he built
a new wall on
that side of it.

You can see now that he had
two nice rooms in his house,
though they weren't very large.
Next, he put in windows to look out of.
He put one window in this room

and he put one
window in that room.

Then he made a tall chimney
on this side of his house.

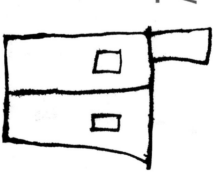

And then he made a tall chimney on the other side of his house.

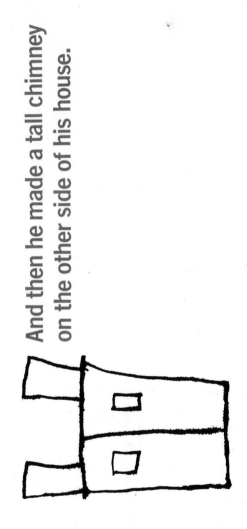

Then he made doors to go in and come out of the house.

He made a door to this room

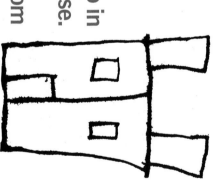

and a door to that room.

After that he built a doorstep in front of the house and he started some grass growing beside it.

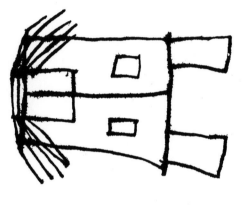

Not far away from
Tommy's house lived a little
girl named Sally.
And there's an

That stands for Sally.

When Tommy had finished his house he thought he would like to go and tell Sally what he had been doing.

So he came
out of his
door and walked along, this way, over to where she lived.

Sally was glad to see him,
and he went into the kitchen and sat down
and explained to her how he had built
two new rooms to his house,
and put in windows and doors,
and made two tall chimneys,
and built a doorstep, and started grass
growing in front of his door.

"And now, Sally," Tommy said, "I want you to come over and see how well I've done everything."

"I'll put on my bonnet and go right back with you," said Sally. But when she was ready to start she said, "Let's go down into the cellar first and get some apples to eat on the way."

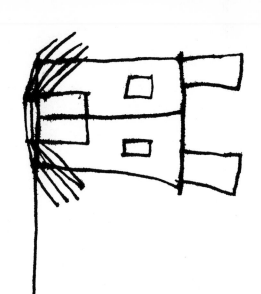

So they went
down into
the cellar,
like this.

They got some apples,
and they came
up outdoors
by the hatchway,
like this.

Now they started for Tommy's house,
but it had rained, and they had only gone
a few steps when they came to a slippery place

and tumbled

down,

like this.

However, they got up quickly, like this.
And they walked along

till they
were nearly to Tommy's
house when they came
to another slippery place,
where they tumbled

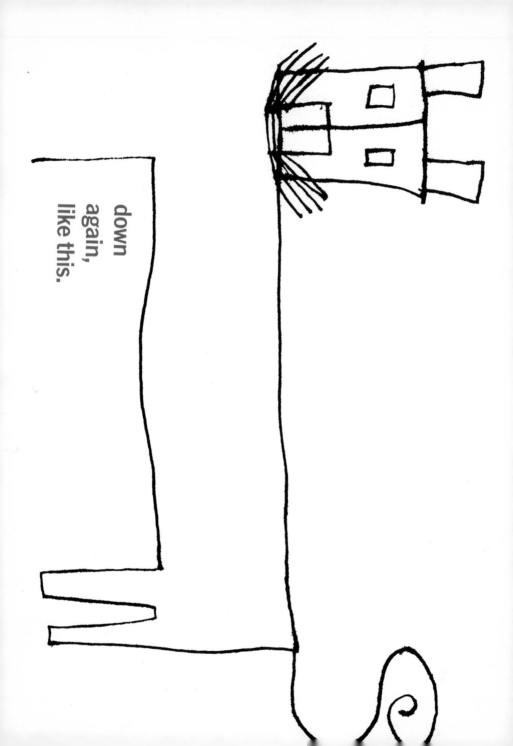

down
again,
like this.

And they were no sooner on their feet, like this,

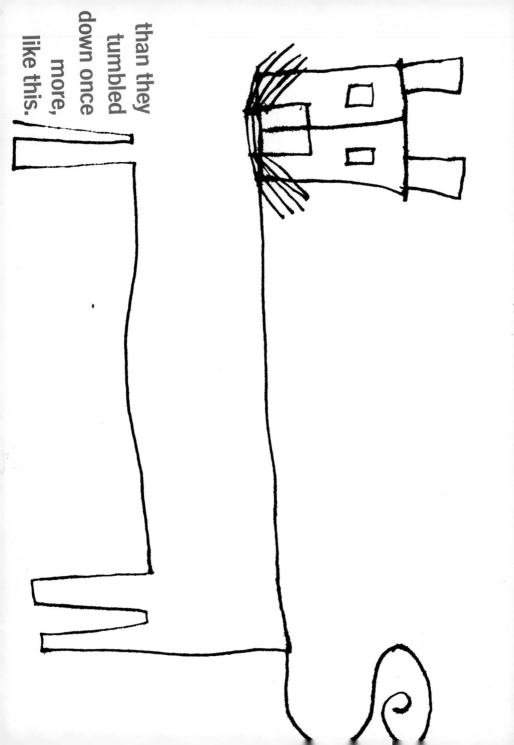

than they
tumbled
down once
more,
like this.

But they were nearly to Tommy's house now, and they got up laughing and were going into the yard straight toward the door, like this—

—when Sally pointed toward the doorstep and cried out,

"O-o-o-o-o-oh! SEE THAT big **Black Cat!**"

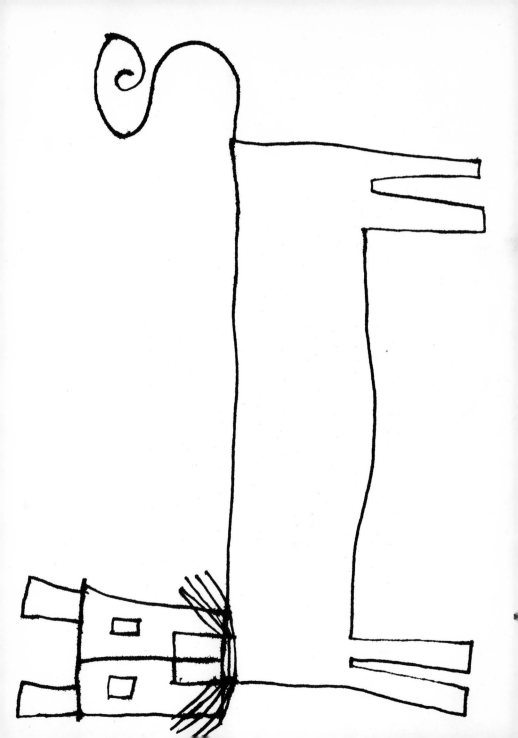

About The Story

The Tale of A Black Cat is a widely known (though rarely printed) drawing story—a kind of folktale which the narrator illustrates as he tells. He creates line by line a single picture, as he develops the story episode by episode. The story invariably has a surprise or trick ending; and the picture is necessarily a simple one which anybody, child or adult, can draw.

Our story follows with some adaptations the version told by Clifton Johnson in The Oak-Tree Fairy Book (Boston, 1905), a volume once popular in all American children's libraries. Clifton Johnson's version, in turn, was an adaptation of a story, "The Black Cat," contributed by Ida C. Craddock to The Journal of American Folklore (X, 1897: 322-323). Miss Craddock had heard the story frequently in childhood, and had recalled it after reading a variant called "Tale of a Wildcat" in an earlier issue (X, 1897: 80) of the same journal.

To the author of Alice In Wonderland we owe another printed variant of our story. Lewis Carroll loved to entertain children with stories, and he mentions several times in his diaries the great success of a story, "Mr. C and Mr. T," which he told to schoolroom groups, illustrating it on a blackboard. Here Mr. C becomes the cat's tail and Mr. T its head (and the house). Instead of Sally and Tommy, the characters are two men, but the story and drawing are basically similar to ours. "Mr. C and Mr. T," with Lewis Carroll's drawing, appears in The Diaries of Lewis Carroll (Roger Lancelyn Green, Editor), New York, 1954, Vol. 2, pp. 572-573.

I hope this book will encourage storytellers young and old to tell this (and other drawing stories) in their own way, and perhaps to invent new ones.

Carl Withers, noted anthropologist and folklorist, is the author of the much-loved I Saw A Rocket Walk A Mile: Nonsense Tales, Chants and Songs from Many Lands and A Rocket In My Pocket: The Rhymes and Chants of Young Americans, as well as several other books for young people.

Mr. Withers' interest in world-wide folklore has kept him at research and at writing in this field for over twenty-five years. The drawing tale here presented is a "by-product" of that research.

Mr. Withers was born in Missouri, attended Harvard College and Columbia University and is now a resident of New York City.

Named by the Artists' Guild as 1965 Artist of the Year, Alan Cober is primarily known for his work in the fields of magazine and advertising illustration. Recently, however, he has taken an interest in the illustration of children's books, and his work for The White Twilight by Madeleine Polland was honored by the Society of Illustrators.

Mr. Cober studied at the Phoenix School of Design, the School of Visual Arts and Pratt Institute. He and his wife and their two young children live in Ossining, New York.